A GOLDEN BOOK • NEW YORK

Cover illustrated by Artful Doodlers

Library of Congress Control Number: 2004114274

ISBN: 0-7364-2351-6

www.goldenbooks.com

www.randomhouse.com/kids/disney

MANUFACTURED IN CHINA

10 9 8 7 6 5 4 3 2

First Edition

12 Princess Stories

CONTENTS

DISNEY'S Aladdin

Illustrated by Phil Ortiz and Serge Michaels

One night, two horsemen raced across the Arabian Desert, chasing a winged medallion. When it stopped, the men watched as the sand rose up to form a huge tiger's head.

"At last—the Cave of Wonders!" Jafar, the Sultan's chief adviser, said to Gazeem. "Bring me the lamp. The rest of the treasure is yours."

As Gazeem stepped into the cave, a ghostly voice boomed, "Only one may enter here! The diamond in the rough." Then the cave's entrance clamped shut, trapping Gazeem inside. The tiger's head quickly dissolved into the sand.

"We must find the diamond in the rough," Jafar said to Iago, his wicked parrot.

The next day, a poor young peasant named Aladdin and his monkey, Abu, were being chased through the marketplace. They had taken a loaf of bread. Aladdin and Abu easily escaped from the palace guards.

Aladdin and Abu could hardly wait to eat, but Aladdin was good-hearted and gave the bread to two hungry children instead. "Someday, Abu, things are going to change," he said. "We'll be rich and live in a palace!"

Meanwhile, at the Sultan's palace, Princess Jasmine was not happy. According to the law, she had to marry a prince by her birthday. "If I do marry," she told her father, "I want it to be for love."

Jasmine was so sad that she decided to run away. Soon she found herself in the marketplace—and in trouble. She took an apple from a cart and gave it to a hungry child.

"You'd better be able to pay for that!" said the fruit seller.

Aladdin dashed up and claimed to be Jasmine's brother. "She's a little crazy," he told the man.

Aladdin and Jasmine tried to get away, but a guard seized Aladdin. "Unhand him!" Jasmine cried.

"Princess Jasmine!" said the guard, surprised. "I would, but my orders come from Jafar."

Jasmine found Jafar and demanded that Aladdin be released.

"Sadly, the boy's sentence has already been carried out—death," Jafar lied.

He knew that Aladdin was the diamond in the rough—the one who was worthy to enter the Cave of Wonders.

Late that night, Jafar disguised himself as an old prisoner in Aladdin's dungeon.

He promised to set Aladdin free and reward him—in return for helping him find a special lamp.

Aladdin agreed. They quickly escaped and hurried off to the Cave of Wonders.

Aladdin and Abu found themselves in a huge cavern filled with coins and jewels. "Just a handful of this stuff would make me richer than the Sultan!" Aladdin exclaimed.

Suddenly, a beautifully woven carpet began floating around them.

"A magic carpet!" cried Aladdin.

The carpet led Aladdin and Abu to a tall staircase. At the top, Aladdin saw the lamp, but just as he reached for it, Abu grabbed a large glittering ruby.

"Abu, no!" shouted Aladdin. But it was too late. The Cave of Wonders began to collapse around them!

Aladdin and Abu survived, but they found themselves trapped inside the dark cave.

"It looks like a beat-up, worthless piece of junk," said Aladdin as he rubbed the lamp. To his astonishment, the lamp began to glow, and an enormous genie emerged!

"You'll grant me any three wishes I want, right?" Aladdin said.

He didn't want to waste one of his wishes, so he tricked the Genie.

"Abu, he probably can't even get us out of this cave," Aladdin teased. To prove his magical power, the Genie helped them escape.

"After I make my first two wishes, I'll use my third wish to set you free," Aladdin promised. But for his first wish, the young man asked, "Can you make me a prince?"

"One prince . . . coming up!" the Genie announced.

Meanwhile, Jafar had come up with a new evil plan. He would hypnotize the Sultan and marry Jasmine!

"You marry the princess—and then you become the Sultan!" Iago squawked.

But before Jafar could finish his spell, the doors of the throne room burst open and a handsome prince entered.

"I have journeyed from afar to seek your daughter's hand in marriage," announced Aladdin, disguised as Prince Ali.

"How dare you!" cried Jasmine. "I am not a prize to be won."

Before Aladdin could respond, Jasmine stormed from the room.

Aladdin, fearing he had lost Jasmine forever, asked the Genie for advice.

"Tell Jasmine the truth," the Genie suggested.

Aladdin had a better idea. He took Jasmine for a ride on the Magic Carpet. During the trip, Jasmine realized that Prince Ali was really the young man from the marketplace.

When Aladdin and Jasmine returned to the palace, they kissed good night. Aladdin realized she cared for him, too.

But seconds later, the palace guards seized Aladdin, tied him up, carried him to a high cliff, and tossed him into the sea.

Using his second wish, Aladdin was saved by the Genie.

Aladdin returned to the palace and revealed Jafar as a traitor.

"Guards!" the Sultan commanded. "Arrest Jafar!"

But Jafar escaped.

"You two will be wed," the Sultan told Jasmine and Aladdin. "And Aladdin will become Sultan!"

Aladdin was worried. He didn't know how to be a sultan! He needed the Genie's help.

"Without you, I'm just Aladdin," he told the disappointed Genie. "I can't wish you free."

Later that day, Jafar had Iago steal the magic lamp. "I wish to rule as Sultan," Jafar commanded, and the Genie had to obey.

For his second wish, Jafar asked to be a powerful sorcerer. He made Jasmine and her father his slaves.

Aladdin realized he couldn't defeat Jafar, so he tricked him instead.

Aladdin convinced Jafar to use his third wish to become a genie. But Jafar had forgotten one very important thing—every genie must be imprisoned in a lamp! With Jafar gone, Aladdin happily made his third wish and freed the Genie.

"You'll always be a prince to me," the grateful Genie told Aladdin.

"And the princess shall marry whomever she wants!" exclaimed the Sultan.

Of course Jasmine chose Aladdin. The young man's greatest wish had come true!

The End

Disney's

Beauty and the Beast

Illustrated by the Disney Storybook Artists

One stormy night, an old beggar woman offered a prince a rose in return for shelter. But the young man was horrified by her appearance and would not let her into his castle.

Suddenly, the woman turned into a beautiful enchantress.

To punish the selfish prince, she changed him into an ugly beast and cast a spell over everyone who lived in the castle. If the Prince could learn to love and be loved in return before the last enchanted rose petal fell, then the terrible spell would be broken. If not, he would remain a beast forever.

In a nearby village lived a beautiful girl named Belle. Gaston the hunter wanted to marry Belle, but unlike all the other girls in the village, Belle didn't like him.

She would rather read her books than listen to Gaston.

Belle's father, Maurice, was an inventor. One morning, he saddled up his faithful horse, Phillipe.

"Good-bye, Belle," said Maurice, kissing his daughter. "I'm off to the fair to show my latest invention."

But Maurice and Phillipe never made it to the fair. They became lost in the dark forest. The howling wolves startled Phillipe. The terrified horse ran off, and Maurice fell from the saddle. The inventor was barely able to escape the wolves! He hid behind a castle gate.

"Not a word," whispered Cogsworth, the clock, to Lumiere, the candlestick, when Maurice entered the castle. The spell had transformed the servants into talking objects!

But the friendly Lumiere said, "Bonjour, monsieur!"

Maurice could not believe his eyes!

Suddenly, a huge beast stormed into the room and growled, "Who are you? Why are you here?"

Before Cogsworth and Lumiere could explain, the Beast grabbed Maurice and threw him into the castle's dungeon.

When Phillipe arrived home without Maurice, Belle knew her father was in trouble. "You have to take me to him!" cried Belle.

They raced for the castle.

At the castle, Belle found her father locked in a cell. They hugged through the bars as Maurice tried to explain what had happened. But soon the Beast appeared.

Belle pleaded with the Beast. "Please let my father go. Take me instead."

The Beast agreed. He threw Maurice out of the castle and then showed Belle to her room. "You can go anywhere you like . . . except the West Wing," he growled.

But Belle could not resist. While exploring the castle, she crept up the stairs to the forbidden West Wing. There she found the enchanted rose. She was about to touch it when the Beast suddenly appeared! "Get out!" he howled.

Terrified, Belle fled the castle and rode away on Phillipe.

Pairs of yellow eyes glowed in the dark forest as a pack of wolves surrounded Belle and Phillipe.

Just as the animals were closing in, the Beast arrived. He fought off the wolves and saved Belle.

Over time, Belle realized that the Beast had a good heart, and the two became friends.

One day, after dancing in the ballroom, the Beast asked Belle if she was happy.

"Yes," Belle sighed. "If only I could see my father again."

The Beast brought Belle a magic mirror. In its reflection, she could see Maurice wandering in the forest, searching for her.

"You must go to him. Take the mirror with you so you'll always have a way to look back and remember me," said the Beast sadly.

Belle found her father and took him home. But their happiness did not last long. Gaston and a group of villagers soon learned about the Beast and set off for the castle to attack him.

When Belle found out, she ran back to the castle. The Beast was badly wounded.

Just as the last enchanted rose petal was about to fall, Belle whispered, "I love you."

With those words, the Beast began to transform. His claws turned into hands and his face grew smooth. The spell was broken! He became a handsome prince again!

Joyfully, all the enchanted objects in the castle returned to their human forms.

Love had saved the day. And Belle and her prince lived happily ever after.

The End

WALT DISNEY'S
Cinderella

**Adapted by Nikki Grimes
Illustrated by Don Williams,
Jim Story, and H. R. Russell**

ne, a wealthy widower lived in
s daughter, Cinderella. He
very much. Still, he felt
have a mother's care, so he
with two young daughters who
inderella's age.

y, the gentleman died soon after, and
ella discovered that her stepmother was a
d cruel woman.

As the years passed, Cinderella's stepmother spoiled her two daughters. Anastasia and Drizella slept in large, lovely bedrooms, but Cinderella was given a tiny room in the attic. And while her stepsisters lived like princesses, poor Cinderella was forced to do laundry, serve meals, and clean house.

Still, Cinderella remained kind and gentle. All the animals loved her. The birds sang to her, and the mice were always there to keep her company. She made tiny clothes for them and often rescued them from the claws of her stepmother's nasty cat, Lucifer.

Early one morning, Cinderella sat at the window in her tiny room and stared out at the castle in the distance. She dreamed of one day wearing a beautiful gown and dancing at a fancy ball. "Someday my dreams will come true," Cinderella said to herself.

Meanwhile, the King wanted his son to marry right away, but the Prince wanted to wait for the girl of his dreams.

The King had an idea. He told the Grand Duke they would have a ball and invite all the young women in the kingdom.

The invitations were delivered that very day.
Cinderella took the invitation from a messenger
and handed it to her stepmother.

As their mother read the invitation aloud,
Anastasia and Drizella jumped with excitement.

Cinderella asked if she could go, too.

"You may go," said her stepmother sternly, "if
you finish all your chores and find something
suitable to wear."

Cinderella ran to her room and found an old ball gown.

"Maybe it's a little old-fashioned, but I'll fix that," she thought, looking at her pattern book. But first she had chores to do, and they seemed never to end!

It was eight o'clock at night when Cinderella completed the last chore—too late to finish her ball gown.

But as she entered her room, there hung her ball gown, finished to look just like the one in the pattern book. The birds and mice had done all the sewing.

"Oh, thank you so much!" Cinderella said.

Cinderella dressed and hurried downstairs to join her stepsisters. But when they saw that she wore a sash and beads that had once belonged to them, Anastasia and Drizella ripped the gown to shreds.

Sobbing, Cinderella ran into the garden.
"It's just no use," she cried. She thought her dreams would never come true.
Suddenly, the garden filled with light, and Cinderella looked up to see her Fairy Godmother.

With a wave of her wand, the Fairy Godmother turned a pumpkin into a glittering coach and the mice into horses. She waved her wand again and changed the horse into a coachman and Bruno the dog into a footman.

Last of all, she transformed Cinderella's rags into a lovely ball gown and put glass slippers on her tiny feet.

Cinderella twirled around in her beautiful new gown. "It's like a dream!" she said with a sigh.

"Yes, my child. But you'll only have until midnight," cautioned her Fairy Godmother. "On the stroke of twelve, the spell will be broken and everything will be as it was before."

At the ball, the Prince rushed over and asked Cinderella to dance. Cinderella smiled and took his hand, never guessing that he was the Prince. They danced all night, and anyone could see that they were falling in love.

Suddenly, the clock began to strike twelve. "Oh, dear! It's midnight! I must leave," said Cinderella, breaking away from the Prince.

"Wait! I don't even know your name! How will I find you?" called the Prince.

The Grand Duke ran after Cinderella. He knew the Prince had finally found the girl he wanted to marry, and the King would be furious if she got away.

Racing down the stairs, Cinderella lost a glass slipper. The Grand Duke, a few steps behind, stopped to pick it up. When he looked around a moment later, she was gone.

Just beyond the palace gates, at the last stroke of midnight, the spell was broken. Just as the Fairy Godmother had said, all was as it had been before. All, that is, except for the tiny glass slipper on Cinderella's foot. She took the slipper off and carried it home.

The next day the King was frantic. "The Prince is determined to marry none but the girl who fits this slipper," the Grand Duke told him.

Cinderella's stepmother decided that Cinderella must not have the chance to try on the slipper. She quickly locked the girl in her room. But Cinderella wasn't locked in for long. The mice stole the key, carried it upstairs, and slipped it under Cinderella's door.

Anastasia and Drizella tried to force their big feet into the tiny slipper, but it was no use.

Then, just as the Grand Duke was about to leave, Cinderella appeared at the top of the stairs. "May I try it on?" she asked.

The footman carried the slipper toward Cinderella, but her stepmother stuck out her cane and tripped him! The glass slipper crashed down onto the floor, shattering into a thousand pieces.

The Grand Duke was horrified.

"But I have the other slipper," Cinderella said with a smile, pulling the glass slipper from under her apron.

The glass slipper slid onto Cinderella's foot. It was a perfect fit!

Soon Cinderella and the Prince were married.
And they lived happily ever after.

The End

DISNEY'S
THE 🐚 LITTLE
MERMAID

Adapted by Stephanie Calmenson
Illustrated by Francesc Mateu

*S*ebastian, the court composer, had planned a royal concert. It was in honor of Triton, the sea king, and all his daughters were to sing. But Ariel, the daughter with the most beautiful voice, hadn't shown up. Triton was losing his patience.

Ariel was busy exploring a sunken ship. The Little Mermaid wanted to know all she could about the creatures called humans.

Ariel held up a fork and cried, "Have you ever seen anything so wonderful in your life?"

"But what is it?" asked her friend Flounder.

Ariel and Flounder went to ask Scuttle the seagull.

"It's a dinglehopper," he said with certainty. "Humans use these little babies to straighten their hair."

Later that day, Ariel was human-watching. She spotted a handsome young man on a ship. As soon as Ariel laid eyes on Prince Eric, she fell in love.

But soon a storm began to rage.

The ship was in trouble! Prince Eric was trying to steer through the storm. The ship's sail caught fire. Rough waves tossed the ship back and forth. Eric went flying into the sea.

"I must save him!" cried Ariel. She dove underwater and pulled the prince ashore.

Prince Eric was still for a very long time. Scuttle wasn't sure if he was alive. But suddenly Ariel saw his chest move up and down. He was breathing!

She began to sing a love song to him but was soon interrupted by Prince Eric's dog, Max.

Ariel hurried back into the water. With Flounder by her side, she headed for home.

When King Triton found out Ariel was in love with a human, he became furious. He destroyed her collection of human objects and told Ariel she could never see the prince again.

Ariel was very sad. She sought out the sea witch, Ursula, for help.

"The only way to get what you want is to become human," Ursula explained.

She would turn Ariel into a human for three days. If Ariel could get the prince to kiss her, she would remain human forever. If not, she would turn back into a mermaid—and belong to Ursula.

But there was a price for Ursula's magic. "What I want from you is your voice!" the evil sea witch demanded.

Because she was in love, Ariel agreed.

With a swirl of her magic potion, Ursula took away Ariel's voice and dropped it into a seashell locket.

Ariel looked down at where her tail used to be. She had legs! Flounder quickly swam her up to the surface.

Prince Eric was fully recovered by the time Flounder dragged Ariel to shore. When the prince saw Ariel, he did not know that she was the one who had saved him. Without her voice, Ariel couldn't sing to him or tell him who she was.

But Prince Eric liked Ariel very much. He took her rowing at twilight. Sebastian tried to help things along. He led Scuttle and his friends in a romantic song.

"Go on! Kiss her!" they cried.

But the prince did not kiss Ariel. Not on the first day, or on the second.

On the third day, Scuttle surprised Ariel with the news that Prince Eric was getting married. He also told her that Vanessa, Prince Eric's bride-to-be, was really Ursula, the sea witch!

Scuttle and his friends rushed the wedding ship and began to attack Vanessa.

Vanessa's seashell locket crashed to the deck, freeing Ariel's voice. When the prince heard Ariel speak, he knew that she was the one who had rescued him. He went to kiss her, but the sun had set. It was too late! Ariel's three days were up!

"We made a deal!" Ursula said. She grabbed Ariel and dove into the sea.

When they reached the ocean floor, King Triton appeared. "Let her go!" he demanded.

"I might be willing to make an exchange for someone even better," Ursula said slyly.

King Triton sadly agreed to the sea witch's bargain. He allowed himself to be turned into a lowly sea creature, and Ariel was set free.

"Now I am the ruler of all the ocean!" shouted Ursula.

Soon Ursula found herself face to face with Prince Eric, who had come to rescue Ariel.

Eric killed wicked Ursula. Triton became the king of the sea once more.

"She really does love him, doesn't she?" Triton asked Sebastian. The crab assured the king. Then, with a wave of his trident, Triton turned Ariel into a human being.

It wasn't long before Prince Eric and Ariel were married. All the creatures on land and sea wished them happiness always.

The End

WALT DISNEY's

Sleeping Beauty

Adapted by Michael Teitelbaum
Illustrated by Sue DiCicco

*I*n a faraway land long ago, King Stefan and his fair queen wished for a child. At last a daughter was born. They named her Aurora and held a great feast to honor the baby princess. Nobles, peasants, knights, and ladies all attended.

King Stefan welcomed his good friend King Hubert to the feast. King Hubert had brought his young son, Phillip, with him. The kings agreed that someday Phillip and Aurora would be married.

Among the guests were three good fairies, Flora, Fauna, and Merryweather. Each of them wished to bless the infant with a gift.

Waving her wand, Flora chanted, "My gift shall be the gift of Beauty."

"And mine," said Fauna, "shall be the gift of Song."

Before Merryweather could speak, the castle doors flew open.

Lightning flashed. Thunder rumbled. A tiny flame appeared and grew into the form of the evil fairy Maleficent and her pet raven.

Maleficent was angry that she hadn't been invited to the feast.

"I, too, have a gift for the newborn babe," she said with a sneer. "Before the sun sets on her sixteenth birthday, she shall prick her finger on the spindle of a spinning wheel . . . and die!"

But Merryweather still had a gift to give. She tried to undo the curse by saying these words to the baby:

"Not in death, but just in sleep
The fateful prophecy you'll keep.
And from this slumber you shall wake
When true love's kiss the spell shall break."

King Stefan ordered that every spinning wheel in the land be burned. But he still feared the evil fairy's curse, so the good fairies took Aurora to live with them, deep in the woods, safe from Maleficent.

The king and queen watched with heavy hearts as the fairies hurried from the castle, carrying the baby princess.

The fairies disguised themselves as peasant women and changed Aurora's name to Briar Rose. The years passed quietly, and Briar Rose slowly grew into a beautiful young woman.

At last the princess reached her sixteenth birthday. Planning a surprise, the fairies sent her out to pick berries. Fauna baked a cake for her while the others sewed her a new gown.

In a mossy glen, Briar Rose danced and sang with her friends, the birds and animals. She told them of her beautiful dream about meeting a tall, handsome stranger and falling in love.

A young man came riding by. When he heard Briar Rose singing, he hid in the bushes to watch her. Then he reached out to take her hand.

Briar Rose was startled. "I didn't mean to frighten you," he said with a smile, "but I feel as though we've met before."

Briar Rose felt very happy. She and her admirer gazed into each other's eyes. The young man didn't know she was Princess Aurora. And she didn't know he was Prince Phillip.

Briar Rose told the fairies that she had fallen in love.

"Impossible!" they cried. They told her the truth at last—that she was a royal princess, betrothed at birth to a prince. And it was time for her to return home. So poor Aurora was led away, still wishing for her handsome stranger.

Maleficent's raven flew off to tell Maleficent that the princess was finally coming home. Using her evil powers, Maleficent lured Aurora to a high tower. There a spinning wheel suddenly appeared.

"Touch the spindle!" urged Maleficent. "Touch it, I say!"

The three good fairies rushed to the rescue, but they were too late. Aurora had touched the sharp spindle and instantly fallen into a deep sleep. Maleficent's curse had come true. Now, with a harsh laugh, the evil fairy vanished.

"King Stefan and the queen will be heartbroken when they find out," said Fauna and Merryweather.

"They're not going to," said Flora. "We'll put them *all* to sleep until the princess awakens." So the three fairies cast a dreamlike spell over everyone in the castle.

Meanwhile, Maleficent had captured Phillip and chained him deep in her dungeon.

But the good fairies had other plans for him. They magically melted his chains. They armed him with the Shield of Virtue and the Sword of Truth. Then they sent him racing to the castle to awaken the princess.

Maleficent hurled heavy boulders at Phillip, but the brave prince rode on.

When he reached Aurora's castle, Maleficent caused a forest of thorns to grow all around it. Phillip hacked the thorns aside with his powerful sword.

In a rage, the evil fairy soared to the top of the highest tower. There she changed into a monstrous dragon. "Now you shall deal with *me,* O Prince!" she shrieked. "And all the Powers of Evil!"

Maleficent breathed fire, but Phillip ducked behind his shield.

Thunder cracked! Flames roared around him! The prince fought bravely. Guided by the good fairies, he threw his magic sword straight as an arrow. It struck the dragon's evil heart. Maleficent was no more.

Phillip raced to the tower where his love lay sleeping. He gently kissed her. The spell was broken. Aurora's eyes slowly opened. Now everyone awoke. The king and queen were overjoyed to see their daughter again.

Wedding plans were soon made. And everyone lived happily ever after!

The End

Walt Disney's

Snow White
and the Seven Dwarfs

Illustrated by Guell

$\mathcal{O}$nce upon a time, there lived a beautiful young princess named Snow White. Her hair was as dark as night, her lips were as red as a rose, and her skin was as white as snow. The Queen was jealous of her, so she dressed Snow White in rags and forced her to scrub the castle.

Each day, the Queen asked her magic mirror, "Magic mirror on the wall, who is the fairest one of all?"

And each day the mirror replied, "You are the fairest one of all."

One day, while Snow White was working in the courtyard, a handsome Prince suddenly appeared. Snow White was so shy that she ran back into the castle. The Prince sang to her through an open window. As she listened, Snow White realized that this was the Prince of her dreams!

The Queen asked, "Magic mirror on the wall, who is the fairest one of all?"

But this time the mirror replied, "Snow White."

In a rage, the Queen summoned the Royal Huntsman and told him to kill Snow White.

The Huntsman led Snow White deep into the forest. But Snow White was so sweet and lovely that he could not bring himself to harm her.

"Run away!" the Huntsman told her. "Hide and never come back."

Snow White raced through the dark woods. Her heart was pounding with fear. A cold wind nipped at her heels. Snow White's dress got caught on a twisted tree branch, and she tripped on a thick root and tumbled to the ground.

Snow White lay there, sobbing. When she dried her tears and looked up, a group of friendly animals stood all around her. The gentle creatures listened to Snow White's sad story, then quickly led her through the woods.

Snow White followed her new friends to a charming little cottage. "It's just like a doll's house!" Snow White exclaimed. "I like it here." And since the door was open, she walked right in.

Inside the cozy cottage were a long wooden table and seven tiny chairs. "There must be seven children living here," said Snow White.

"If we clean the place up," Snow White told her animal friends, "perhaps they'll let me stay!"

So they made the room as clean as could be; then Snow White explored the rest of the cottage.

Snow White found a big room with seven little beds. Each bed had a name carved on it: Doc, Happy, Sneezy, Dopey, Grumpy, Bashful, and Sleepy.

"What funny names for children," Snow White thought as she lay down across three of the beds to sleep.

That night, the owners of the cottage returned. But they weren't seven little children—they were the Seven Dwarfs! When they saw their clean and tidy house, the Dwarfs immediately knew something strange was going on.

All Seven Dwarfs crept upstairs and found Snow White stretching and yawning under the sheets. They thought she was a monster!

"Let's attack it while it's sleepin'," Doc said.

But just then Snow White popped her head out and said, "How do you do?"

By the time Snow White had finished her sad story, the Dwarfs wanted her to stay.

"We'll protect you from the Queen," they told Snow White.

At the castle, the evil Queen learned that Snow White was still alive. So she decided to get rid of the girl once and for all.

The Queen made a potion that would transform her into an ugly old hag.

Then, using a book of magic, the evil Queen created a poison apple.

"One taste and Snow White's eyes will close forever!" she cackled.

There was only one cure for the Queen's sleeping spell—true love's first kiss.

That night, Snow White and the Seven Dwarfs were singing, dancing, and making merry. Before they went to sleep, Snow White told the Dwarfs a bedtime story—all about the handsome Prince of her dreams.

Early the next morning, Snow White made breakfast and gave each Dwarf a kiss on the forehead as he left to work in the diamond mines.

"Beware of strangers," the Dwarfs warned. Then they marched off, cheerfully singing.

As Snow White began her chores, an ugly old woman suddenly appeared.

She gave Snow White a big red apple. "They're delicious, dearie," she cooed.

Snow White's animal friends didn't like the old woman, but kindly Snow White invited her inside.

"This is a magic wishing apple," the old woman said. "One bite and all your dreams will come true."

Snow White took a bite of the apple and fell to the floor. Her animal friends raced off to find the Seven Dwarfs.

The Dwarfs arrived just as the hag was leaving. They chased her through the woods and up a rocky cliff. Higher and higher she climbed, with the Dwarfs close behind. When she reached the top, lightning struck where she was standing, and the hag went shrieking over the edge.

The Seven Dwarfs found Snow White in a deep, deep sleep. They vowed to watch over her forever.

It wasn't long before the Prince, who had been searching far and wide for the fair Snow White, rode up to the cottage.

The Prince knelt beside the sleeping Snow White. Then he leaned down and kissed her. Snow White's eyes fluttered open. She was alive! The Seven Dwarfs danced with joy.

Then the Prince lifted Snow White onto his white horse and they rode off together—to live happily ever after.

The End

Disney's Beauty and the Beast

Getting to Know You

By Lisa Ann Marsoli

Illustrated by the Disney Storybook Artists

"Maybe the Beast has a heart after all," thought Belle after he rescued her from a pack of wolves. Even though the Beast was angry with Belle for leaving the castle, he had risked his own life to save hers.

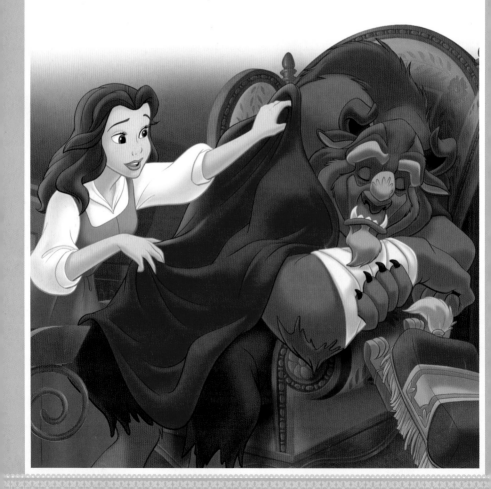

Mrs. Potts, Lumiere, and Cogsworth were hopeful. If the Beast and Belle fell in love, the spell that enchanted them would be broken—and they would all become human again!

"Master," said Mrs. Potts to the Beast, "why not have a nice hot drink in front of the fireplace? I'm sure Belle would love some company."

The Beast stomped into the sitting room and settled himself in a chair by the fireplace.

Belle looked up from her book. "Good evening," she said.

The Beast did his best to smile politely.

Belle went back to her reading until she was startled by a loud slurp. She glanced at the Beast and saw that he had a hot-chocolate mustache. He was messy as well as noisy!

The Beast stopped drinking, wiped his face, and slumped unhappily in his chair.

"Why don't I read you a story?" Belle suggested. She read the Beast a story filled with fire-breathing dragons and brave knights. The Beast sat on the edge of his seat, listening to every word. And when he drank his cocoa, he took care to sip instead of slurp.

The next day, Lumiere and Cogsworth decided to play matchmaker, too.

"What a beautiful day for a walk!" Cogsworth said after breakfast.

And before Belle and the Beast could protest, they were bundled into winter capes and gloves and herded outdoors.

The couple walked along in uncomfortable silence. Then they came to a mud puddle.

"A gentleman would carry me over," Belle thought. Clearly, the Beast wasn't a gentleman.

"Oh, well, here goes!" she thought as she waded through the mud.

Soon the wind picked up, and it started to snow.

The Beast gently took Belle's hand and led her through the blizzard.

Lumiere and Cogsworth were watching out the window as the two approached, holding hands. It looked so romantic!

"It seems as if you and the Master are getting to know each other better," said Mrs. Potts.

"I suppose," Belle answered. "There is so much about him that's gruff and rude—yet he's full of surprises."

In another part of the castle, the Beast told Cogsworth, "Belle can be rather boring and proper. But then she walked through the mud without complaining. And she didn't act scared at all when we were caught in the storm. She's full of surprises."

"Remember, Master," Lumiere coached before lunch, "young ladies appreciate politeness."

Once settled at the table, Belle and the Beast tried to smile, but both were tired from trying so hard to get along with each other.

The Beast picked up a chicken leg and began to devour it. But after Belle placed her napkin in her lap, he hurriedly grabbed his own napkin and did the same.

"Isn't this lunch delicious?" asked Belle.

"Mmpffgrl," answered the Beast, his mouth stuffed with food.

Then, when the Beast ducked down to get his napkin, which had fallen on the floor, he tipped the table over! A roll soared across the table toward Belle.

To the Beast's surprise, she pitched the roll right back at him!

When Mrs. Potts, Lumiere, and Cogsworth came in, they couldn't believe their eyes. The room was a mess, and even more peculiar, Belle and the Beast were laughing!

Mrs. Potts said, "I think they discovered what we forgot: the best way to make friends is to relax and be yourself!"

Later that night, Belle patiently taught the Beast how to dance. He listened carefully to everything she told him, and soon the two were gliding across the dance floor . . . in step with each other at last.

The End

DISNEY'S THE LITTLE MERMAID

A Whale of a Time

By Irene Trimble
Illustrated by Darryl Goudreau

One day, Ariel and Flounder were looking for treasures under the sea.

Suddenly, Flounder stopped and said, "Ariel, do you hear something?"

"Like what?" Ariel asked.

"Like THAT!" Flounder cried, pointing to a large shape making squeaky noises.

Ariel moved closer for a better look.

"Hey!" she said, beaming. "It's a whale—an adorable baby gray whale!"

"But where's the baby's family?" Ariel asked. "This little guy must be lost. We should take him to the palace right away."

"Yes, King Triton will know what to do," Flounder said.

At the palace, King Triton knew exactly what to do. "I'll send out a search party to look for the whale's family," Triton told Ariel and Flounder. "You two can take care of him until we find them."

As Ariel and Flounder happily swam off with the baby whale, Sebastian the crab called after them, "Have fun babysitting!"

The babysitters found a school of angelfish that wanted to play tag. But when the baby whale flapped his giant tail—WHOOSH—every angelfish behind him went flying!

"Maybe you're too big for this game," Ariel said with a laugh.

"Let's play hide-and-seek!" Flounder suggested.

But the baby whale couldn't find anything big enough to hide behind.

"We'll find some other way to have fun," Ariel told the whale.

"I know," Ariel said. "You can come with me to singing rehearsal at the palace!"

But when they reached the stage door, the baby whale just couldn't fit through.

"Don't be sad," Ariel told him. "You can watch from here."

The baby whale loved the chorus! In fact, he loved it so much that he joined in the singing. But the whale's song was so loud that everyone else's voice was drowned out.

"I think your voice is a little too loud for our chorus," Ariel said gently as she helped the baby out of the doorway. "Come on, Flounder. Help me take him outside."

The whale kept singing happily as they left the palace.

"Ariel, I hear something in the distance," Flounder said. "And it's coming closer!"

"Why, it sounds like the baby whale's song, but even louder!" Ariel cried.

"Look!" cried Flounder as two huge whales swam toward them.

"It's the baby whale's parents! They must have heard him singing," Ariel exclaimed.

The little gray whale answered his parents with squeaks and squeals of joy.

King Triton ordered that a celebration be held in honor of the happy reunion. All the creatures of the sea joined in. The sea horses rocked, the starfish shimmied, and the puffer fish puffed. And, of course, the whales sang their happiest song.

Hours later, the celebration was over, and the whale family waved good-bye and swam off.

"You know," Flounder said, "for a little baby, he sure was a BIG handful."

"Yes, he was," Ariel agreed. "But taking care of him together was also BIG fun!"

The End

Adapted by Katherine Poindexter
Illustrated by José Cardona
and Don Williams

${M}$any years ago in China, there lived a young woman named Fa Mulan. Mulan tried to be like all the other girls—but she was not always graceful.

Poor Mulan accidentally poured tea all over the woman who was to find her a husband.

"You will never bring your family honor!" the Matchmaker snapped.

Mulan loved her parents very much, and she couldn't bear to disappoint them.

Her father only smiled. "What beautiful blossoms we have this year," he said, looking at the trees. "But look—one is late. I'll bet when it blooms, it will be the most beautiful of all."

That night Mulan sneaked into her parents' room. She took her father's notice to report to the army. In its place she left the beautiful comb she had worn in her hair.

With her father's sword, Mulan cut her long, dark hair. Then she slipped into his armor. She would pretend to be a young man and fight in place of her father.

Mulan knew the danger. But she loved her father too much to let him go to war.

In the family temple, the Fa Family Ancestors awakened. "If they discover Mulan is a girl," said the First Ancestor, "she will bring shame to her family. We must send the most powerful Guardian to bring her home."

When the little dragon Mushu offered to go, the First Ancestor laughed and said, "You are not worthy. Awaken the Great Stone Dragon!"

Mushu tried to wake the mighty Guardian by banging on his ear—but the Great Stone Dragon crumbled into a pile of rocks!

Quickly, Mushu decided to find Mulan on his own. He would do more than just bring her home—he'd make her a hero and regain his position as Guardian in the Fa Family Temple!

Mushu caught up with Mulan. He let Cri-Kee the cricket come, too. Crickets were known to bring good luck, and Mulan certainly needed that!

"Walk like a man," said Mushu. But Mulan was stumped when her new captain, Li Shang, asked her name. "My name? It's a boy's name, sir. It's, uh, Ping," she replied.

Mulan trained long and hard with the other recruits. The most challenging task of all was to retrieve an arrow from the top of a tall pole. Not a single recruit was able to do it! But Mulan used strength and discipline to accomplish the task.

Once they had finished training, Mulan and the other soldiers marched into the mountains to face the Huns. Led by the evil Shan-Yu, the Huns launched a surprise attack and showered Shang's army with flaming arrows. Then the villains charged toward Shang's troops.

"Aim the last cannon at Shan-Yu!" Shang cried. But Mulan had a different plan. She grabbed the cannon and ran toward the attacking Huns. Then she lit the cannon's fuse.

KABOOM! The rocket flew into the snowy mountainside, causing an avalanche of snow to bury Shan-Yu and all the evil Huns.

As the avalanche raced down the mountainside, Mulan found Shang buried in the snow. With a great heave, she pulled him onto her horse and carried him to safety.

"Let's hear it for Ping!" one of the soldiers shouted. "The bravest of us all!"

Suddenly, Mulan held her side in pain. "Ping is wounded! Get help!" Shang cried.

After tending to Mulan, the doctor stepped out of the medical tent and whispered to Shang. Shang stepped back in shock. Ping was a woman! Under Chinese law, the penalty for such a grave lie was death!

Shang was hurt and angry at Mulan's lies. But she had saved his life, so in return he spared hers. Shang and his army rode off for the Imperial City, leaving Mulan behind.

"I never should have come," Mulan said to Mushu. Sadly, she prepared to go home.

Suddenly, Mulan saw that a handful of Huns had survived the battle—including Shan-Yu. They were heading for the Imperial City to attack the Emperor! Mulan knew she had to do something.

Mulan raced to the Imperial City, where she found Shang and his soldiers. "The Huns are alive!" she cried. "And they're here!"

"Why should I believe you?" Shang replied coldly as he rode past her. Mulan tried to warn others in the crowd. But no one listened.

All too soon they saw that Mulan was telling the truth. Shan-Yu captured the Emperor and held him prisoner. But Mulan had an idea! She dressed three of the soldiers up with wigs, makeup, and paper fans. The Huns paid no attention when some "young ladies" appeared in the palace.

As Shang fought with Shan-Yu, Mulan and her friends helped the Emperor escape.

Shan-Yu knocked Shang unconscious and began chasing Mulan. As she ran, Mulan spotted the tower where the Emperor's fireworks were stored. With one look from Mulan, Mushu figured out how he could help.

Mulan led Shan-Yu on a wild chase throughout the palace and onto the roof, where she bravely faced him. Just then, Mushu arrived—with a rocket on his back! Cri-Kee lit the fuse, and Mushu jumped off just as the rocket struck Shan-Yu and carried him straight to the fireworks tower. KABOOM!

As smoke from the explosion drifted away, the Emperor appeared. To Mulan's surprise, he bowed to her and said, "You have saved us all." Then he gave Mulan two gifts: Shan-Yu's sword and a pendant bearing the Emperor's royal crest.

When Mulan arrived home, she presented the Emperor's gifts to her father. Fa Zhou accepted them with pride but quickly set them aside and gathered Mulan in his arms. "The greatest gift and honor," he said with a smile, "is having you for a daughter."

Moments later, Shang arrived.

Mulan asked Shang to stay for dinner. Shang smiled and nodded.

At the same time, the First Ancestor said to Mushu, "You can be Guardian again."

"Yippee!" shouted Mushu. He and Cri-Kee were lucky to know someone as wonderful as Mulan!

The End

DISNEY'S
THE LITTLE MERMAID

Make-believe Bride

By K. Emily Hutta
Illustrated by the Disney Storybook Artists

riel's secret grotto was her favorite place in the whole undersea world—especially now that a statue of Prince Eric was there.

"Oh, Flounder, it's almost like having Eric with me!" Ariel said with a sigh.

"Get ahold of yourself," cried Sebastian. "That's nothing but a hunk of rock!"

Ariel placed her head on the statue's shoulder. "Why, yes, I'd love to marry you, Eric," she said, pretending.

"*Marry?*" Sebastian roared.

"It's a statue, remember?" Ariel said. "I'm just playing make-believe."

"We can have the wedding right here," Ariel continued. "You both can help me!"

"Help you with what?" Sebastian asked as Ariel showered him with decorations.

"Oh, dream weddings are every bit as much work as real weddings," Ariel said.

"I think Prince Eric is dressed perfectly for a wedding," Ariel said, looking lovingly at the statue. "But I'll need something fancier to wear!"

"Flounder, you can be the chef," said Ariel. "I want you to prepare the most wonderful foods you can imagine."

"Seaweed soufflé . . . plankton pie . . . ," Flounder suggested. "Just leave it to me!"

"And don't forget the wedding cake!" Ariel cried.

"Oh, I can hardly wait!" Ariel exclaimed. "I can picture the entire ceremony. My sisters will make such beautiful bridesmaids. And my father will be so proud as we—"

"Your father?" Sebastian looked as if he was ready to faint.

"Oh, don't be such a party pooper, Sebastian," Ariel said lightly. "Remember . . . it's all just pretend."

"I'm leaving," Sebastian said. "I can't take any more of this nonsense."

"Now I'll have to ask someone else to conduct the wedding's grand orchestra," said Ariel.

"Grand orchestra?" Sebastian asked, stopping in his tracks.

"A crab must do what a crab must do!" Sebastian cried. "The show—er, rather, the wedding—must go on!"

Flounder brought Ariel a beautiful string of pearls. "They belong to a friend," Flounder said. "You can borrow them."

Now Ariel had something old (the dinglehopper to comb her hair), something new (her veil), something borrowed (the pearls), and something blue (her blue shell bracelet).

The next morning, Sebastian scuttled after Ariel as she swam from the palace.

"I hope no one sees us," Sebastian said nervously. "It might be hard to explain where you're going dressed like this!"

Flounder escorted Ariel into the grotto.

"Dum-dum-de-dum, dum-dum-de-dum . . ." Sebastian sang the wedding march as his orchestra played. He stopped when Ariel passed and wailed, "Weddings always make me cry!"

Sebastian cleared his throat importantly. "Do you, Princess Ariel, take this . . . er . . . statue to be your make-believe husband?"

"I do!" Ariel declared.

"And do you, Mr. Pretend Prince, take this princess to be your make-believe wife?" Sebastian went on.

"He says he does," Ariel said with a giggle.
"Well, then, I pronounce you imaginary
husband and wife," Sebastian said.

Ariel hugged her friends. "Oh, thank you! This
has been a wonderful dream wedding!" she cried.
"And now I'm inviting you both to my *real*
wedding to Prince Eric. I'm not sure when, or
where, or how, but I know it *will* happen. Nothing
can stand in the way of true love!"

Ariel sighed with happiness, imagining a kiss from Prince Eric.

"Yikes!" she cried. She realized she was actually kissing a very startled Flounder!

"Aha!" Sebastian shouted. "See what comes of silly notions about marrying human princes! As if that could ever really happen . . ."

The End

Disney's
Beauty and the BEAST

Friends Are Sweet

By Jennifer Liberts
Illustrated by Darrell Baker

$\mathcal{H}$ello, my name is Chip. I'm a teacup. My best friend is a very smart girl named Belle. We have lots of fun adventures together, but yesterday's takes the cake . . . well, the cupcake, actually!

It was Mama's birthday, and all her friends in the castle were busy planning a surprise party. Belle and I decided to make a sweet treat.

Belle turned toward the cupboards and said, "Who wants to help make cupcakes for Mrs. Potts?" Suddenly, the whole kitchen came alive! Everyone wanted to help!

Belle and I mixed the ingredients together and poured the batter into the cupcake tin.

We put the cupcakes in the oven and asked Cogsworth, the mantel clock, to let us know when they were done baking.

After the cupcakes cooled, Belle and I started decorating them. That was when I realized we'd forgotten something.

"Belle, we didn't ask Lumiere if he'd light the birthday candles," I said.

"Where is Lumiere?" asked Belle. "I haven't seen him all morning."

"Perhaps he's in the Master's quarters," Cogsworth suggested.

"Yes," Belle said, "maybe Lumiere is lighting his fireplace."

Belle and I went to the Master's quarters, but Lumiere wasn't there.

"Have you seen Lumiere?" I asked the Featherduster.

"No. Just a lot of dust bunnies," she said.

Next, Belle and I went to look in her bedroom. But we didn't find Lumiere there, either.

"We can't find Lumiere," I said to the Footstool. "Have you seen him?"

The Footstool wagged its tassels and ran to the door.

"I think he knows where Lumiere is!" cried Belle.

We followed the Footstool to the library.

"In here?" I asked the Footstool. He wagged his tassels some more and began sniffing around.

"I don't see him," Belle said sadly.

Suddenly, out of the corner of my eye, I saw some drops of wax on the floor.

"Look, Belle!" I called. "He was here! He was here!"

"If we follow the wax, we should find Lumiere," said Belle.

The drops of wax led down a cold, dark hallway. There were spiderwebs everywhere.

We continued to follow the wax. The hallway
got darker and colder.

"I'm freezing! And it's so dark I can hardly see
my handle," I whispered to Belle.

"Look," Belle said softly. "There's a light up
ahead."

Belle was right!

"The light is coming from under that door!" I shouted. We ran toward it. Belle turned the doorknob and pulled, but she couldn't open the door.

"Lumiere?" called Belle. "Are you in there?"

"Mademoiselle? Is that you?" shouted Lumiere from the other side of the door. "I've been stuck in this closet for hours. I was looking for decorations for the party when the wind slammed the door and locked me in!"

Belle rushed to close the window. Then the two of us pulled with all our might. The door finally popped open.

"Thank you, Monsieur Chip," said a relieved Lumiere. "Thank you, Mademoiselle."

"Now you can light Mama's birthday candles— that's your special job!" I said.

Everyone was happy to see Lumiere.

"You're just in time to light the candles," announced Cogsworth. "Mrs. Potts is on her way!"

As Mama entered the room, we all yelled, "Surprise! Happy birthday!"

Mama was so excited she almost flipped her lid.

Mama thanked us for the cupcakes, and Lumiere told her how Belle and I had rescued him.

Belle gave me a kiss on the cheek. "I couldn't have found Lumiere without your help," she told me.

The cupcakes were sweet, but nothing's sweeter than my best friend, Belle!

The End

DISNEY's Aladdin

One True Love

By Annie Auerbach
Illustrated by the Disney Storybook Artists

"*I*'m baaack!" called the Genie. "How's my favorite couple?"

"We've missed you," said Aladdin. "How was your trip around the world?"

"Fabulous!" the Genie replied. "I saw the pyramids in Egypt and worked on my tan in the Caribbean. A nice shade of blue, don't you think?"

Suddenly, Aladdin and Jasmine were surrounded by gifts from every country the Genie had visited! He had a special surprise for Aladdin.

"A kangaroo?" Aladdin gasped as his gift leaped over the palace wall. "I'd better go catch it!"

"Oh, Genie, it's good to have you back," said Jasmine. "But why do you look so sad?"

"I got a bit lonely while traveling," he said. "I wish I could find a genie to share my life with."

"I know how that can feel," Jasmine said. "Remember, I went through a lot of suitors before I found my one true love.

"I told my father that I wanted to marry for love," Jasmine added. "But the law stated that I had to marry a prince. My father had every suitor he could find come and court me."

"Sounds like you were pretty popular!" the Genie said.

"Popular? Yes. Happy? No!" said Jasmine.

"At first, I tried to make the best of the situation," Jasmine said. "Brand-new colorful outfits were ordered for me. It was fun in the beginning, trying on one beautiful dress after another—"

"You must have looked gorgeous, *dahling*!" interrupted the Genie.

"My father had ordered more than just new outfits," Jasmine said.

But the clothes and jewelry didn't keep Jasmine happy for long. "The suitors my father sent to court me were all wrong," she explained. "No amount of jewelry could make me like those princes!

"First, there was the one I called Prince Achoo," said Jasmine. "He said hello—and sneezed. He handed me flowers—and sneezed. When he realized he was allergic to everything in the palace, he ran off!

"As the days passed, each suitor seemed worse than the one before," Jasmine continued. "Prince Macho told me he wanted a wife to do all his cooking and cleaning. I told him I wanted a husband who wasn't living in the Stone Age!

"Next was Prince Wishy-Washy," said Jasmine. "He didn't have an opinion on anything! When I asked him what he wanted for lunch, he said he would eat whatever I liked. So I told him we were having roasted ant pitas with rat hummus! I guess he didn't like the sound of that!

"When Prince Ali came to my balcony, I told him I was tired of being forced to meet all the suitors," Jasmine explained. "He said I should be free to make my own choice!"

Soon after, Jasmine discovered that Prince Ali was Aladdin in disguise. And no law could keep true love from blossoming. . . .

"Genie? Genie! What's wrong?" Jasmine asked.

The Genie was bawling like a baby. "That was the sweetest story I've ever heard!"

Jasmine laughed. "Genie, you can find the same happiness that Aladdin and I share. I know your special genie is out there!"

Just then, Aladdin showed up with the kangaroo.

"No time to talk, Al," said the Genie. "I've got a genie to find—and not a thing to wear!"

"He wants what we have," said Jasmine, kissing Aladdin on the cheek. "True love."

The Genie reappeared and did a quick fashion show for Jasmine and Aladdin. "Do I go for the handsome banker look? Or perhaps the surfer look?" the Genie asked.

"You want someone to like you because of who you are on the inside," Jasmine said. "Just be yourself."

A lightbulb went on above the Genie's head. "Presto change-o!" he said, and all the new clothes vanished. "How do you like my new . . . er . . . old look?"

"It fits perfectly," Jasmine said warmly.

After the Genie had left, Aladdin took Jasmine on a Magic Carpet ride. Suddenly, she saw a basket of food and a blanket on a nearby mountaintop.

"Our own private picnic!" said Jasmine. "Oh, Aladdin! I'm so lucky to have you!"

Aladdin shook his head. "No, *I'm* the lucky one."

Jasmine was grateful for the gift of true love she had finally found with Aladdin.

"Well, Jasmine," said Aladdin, "it's been quite a day."

"And there's no one I'd rather end it with than you," Jasmine told him with a smile.

The End